# ANNO'S ITALY
## Mitsumasa Anno

**COLLINS**

**Other Picture Books By Mitsumasa Anno**

ANNO'S ANIMALS
THE KING'S FLOWER
ANNO'S JOURNEY

*Library of Congress Cataloging in Publication Information is at the end of book*

Copyright © 1978 by Fukuinkan Shoten Publishers, Tokyo. Japanese edition entitled MY JOURNEY II by Mitsumasa Anno. First United States edition 1980, William Collins Publishers, Inc., New York and Cleveland. All rights reserved. Printed in Japan.

ANNO
1978

## A note about the pictures

There are figures from many well-known stories, films, paintings, and sculptures in the pictures in this book, as well as references to both the Old Testament and the New Testament of the Bible. Readers may also recognize references to great architectural achievements and famous landmarks. Listed here are some things to watch for. See how many others you can find.

Pinocchio, the Three Little Pigs, the Ugly Duckling, Ali Baba, Cinderella, *Primavera* (after Botticelli), *The Annunciation* (after Fra Angelico), *The Last Supper* (after Leonardo da Vinci), *Pieta* (after Michelangelo); the Ponte dei Sospiri (Venice), the Ponte Vecchio (Florence), the cathedral of Santa Maria della Salute (Venice), the Fontana di Trevi (Rome); Strega Nona, Tarzan, and William Shakespeare's *The Merchant of Venice*.

## Author's note

"How is it that, although you are Japanese, you understand so well the history and cultural heritage of Europe?" This is a question I am often asked by Europeans, who look back with nostalgia in their eyes to the golden days when there were as yet no cars on the streets of their villages and cities. In answer, I like to tell about a wedding ceremony which I happened to see near Füssen in West Germany. As I stood at the back of the church, listening to the peaceful melody of the processional hymn, I saw the bridal party come into the church. Watching the ceremony, it was easy for me to pick out the bride and the bridegroom and their parents, as well as the bridesmaid and the best man and their friends. Among them I distinguished the mother of the bride at a glance, for she was wiping away her tears, again and again. It seems that, although languages, alphabets and customs are different in the various parts of the world, there are no differences at all in our hearts, especially when we are shedding tears at parting. What trifles the formal differences are, when you think of what our hearts have in common!

The laws of physics and nature are universal, as are the principles of plant and animal life throughout the world. Among living creatures, more things are shared than are different. Seeing a sunset in Europe, I was impressed by the natural truth that we have only one sun—that, no matter where we are, we all see the same sun.

Although it is difficult for me to understand the languages of the western world, still I can understand the hearts of the people. This book has no words, yet I feel sure that everyone who looks at it can understand what the people in the pictures are doing, and what they are thinking and feeling.

—*Mitsumasa Anno*

**Library of Congress Cataloging in Publication Data**

Anno, Mitsumasa, 1926-    Anno's Italy.

SUMMARY: Records in drawings the artist's journey in Italy, with the theme of the life of Christ interwoven with the
daily activities of the people.

[1. Italy—Pictorial works. 2. Stories without words] I. Title. II. Title: Italy.

PZ7.A5875Aq    [E]    79-17649    ISBN 0-529-05559-7    ISBN 0-529-05560-0 lib. bdg.